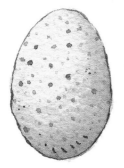

P9-DDI-196

For Mike and our Hesterbrood:
Nick, Caroline, and Teddy
and my parents, the bird-watchers –K.H.

To Audrey Marie –S.R.

NANCY PAULSEN BOOKS
an imprint of Penguin Random House LLC
375 Hudson Street
New York, NY 10014

Text copyright © 2018 by Katie Hesterman.
Illustrations copyright © 2018 by Sergio Ruzzier.

Penguin supports copyright. Copyright fuels creativity, encourages diverse voices,
promotes free speech, and creates a vibrant culture. Thank you for buying an authorized edition of this book and
for complying with copyright laws by not reproducing, scanning, or distributing any part of it in any form without
permission. You are supporting writers and allowing Penguin to continue to publish books for every reader.

Nancy Paulsen Books is a registered trademark of Penguin Random House LLC.

Library of Congress Cataloging-in-Publication Data is available upon request.

Manufactured in China by RR Donnelley Asia Printing Solutions Ltd.
ISBN 9780399547782
10 9 8 7 6 5 4 3 2 1

Design and title lettering by Jaclyn Reyes.
Text set in ShagExpert Mystery and ShagExpert Exotica.
The art was done in pen and ink and watercolor.

A Round of Robins

KATIE HESTERMAN · ILLUSTRATED BY **SERGIO RUZZIER**

NANCY PAULSEN BOOKS

R0451877747

CHEERY-UP, CHEERIO, CHEERIO, CHEERIO!

Turf Tune

Defender Dad sings, "Back away,
'Cause Mom and I are here to stay!
We'll raise a brood, and when we're done,
We just might hatch another one."

Home Sweet Home

Mama is an architect;
With skill and patience, she'll collect
Bits of twig, string, wool, and hair
To form a tiny, twiney lair.

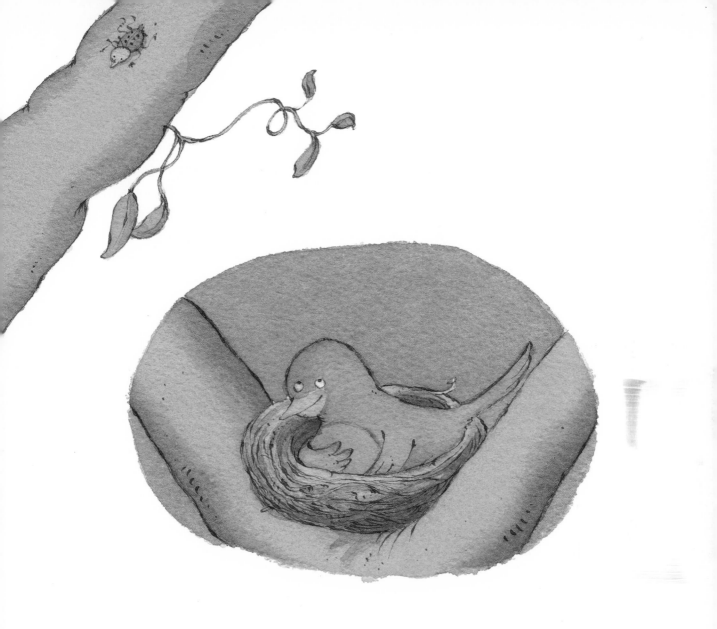

Sweet soft grass lines Mama's bowl.

A muddy middle keeps it whole.

It's guaranteed a perfect fit

So all she has to do is sit.

EGGcessories

Three is too few.

Mama adds more.

Now it's just right:

One clutch of four.

Red-Hot Mama

A heater hides on Mama's chest
To warm each egg inside her nest.
With sensors set at incubake,
In just a dozen days she'll make
Four little ones all set to hatch—

An up-and-coming birdie batch.

Inside Job

Head and tail,
Beak and feather,
Closely cramped
All together.

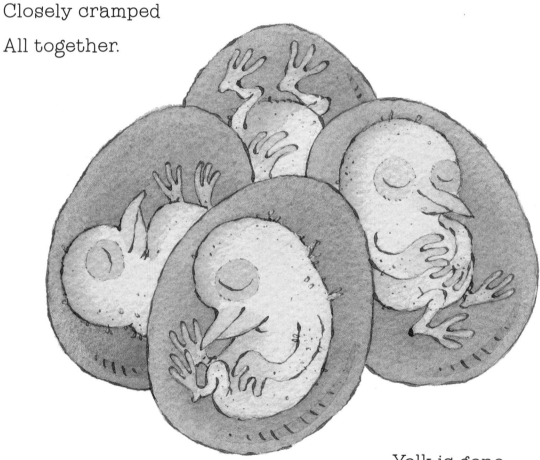

Yolk is gone.
Space is tight.
Pack it in
One more night.

Welcome to the World

Pip, pip, an eggshell chip.

Peck, peck, a bright blue fleck.

Tweak, tweak, a peeking beak,

C-R-R-R-A-C-K-E-D...

All unpacked!

Full House

Beaks wide open, eyes closed tight,
Wobble, bobble, heads upright.
Patchy bodies missing feathers
Huddle-cuddle close together.

Everybirdy Sleeps

Mama's feathers dim the light.

Drowsy darlings snuggle tight.

Balmy breezes rustle tree.

Babies slumber blissfully.

Food Fight

Jumble, jostle, rumble, squirm;
Dad has landed with a worm.
Game of tug-of-war begins—
Biggest bossy baby wins.

PEEP-PEEP-PEEP-PEEP!

Almost a Fledgling

Sleeping, eating, then repeating,

Heading in the right direction.

Changing, growing and it's showing . . .

Now they're fluffs of plump perfection.

YEEEEP TUK-TUK-TUK-TUK

Pop Patrol

A high-speed chase
Is under way.
Dad swoops, then strikes–
He'll make them pay.

To crows and jays
Dad sends a shout:
"Invade my space,
I'll bounce you out."

Just Wing It

Beaks reach to sky.

Wings flap-flap try.

One, two, three,

F
  L
    Y

Fledgling Fill-Up

Wiggle, whip

Squiggle, slip

Wobble, sup

Gobble, up

Worms!

Pool Party

Speckled plumpies thrash about,
Hopping, plopping in and out.
Basking in a birdy pool—
Sorry, sparrows; robins rule!

Earning Their Wings

Fledglings' spots are fading fast.
Baby days have quickly passed.
Romping robins roam the lawn,
Hunting till the worms are gone.
Zipping through the 'hood in flight,
Roosting with their flock at night—
On their own, they'll be all right!

Here They Grow Again

Empty nesters? Not so soon.

Dad retweets his tough turf tune.

Mama builds her second lair,

Plucks and tucks with utmost care.

Eggs? You bet, she lays four more.

Turquoise blue, just like before.

Then, in just a dozen days . . .

Welcome to the world replays!

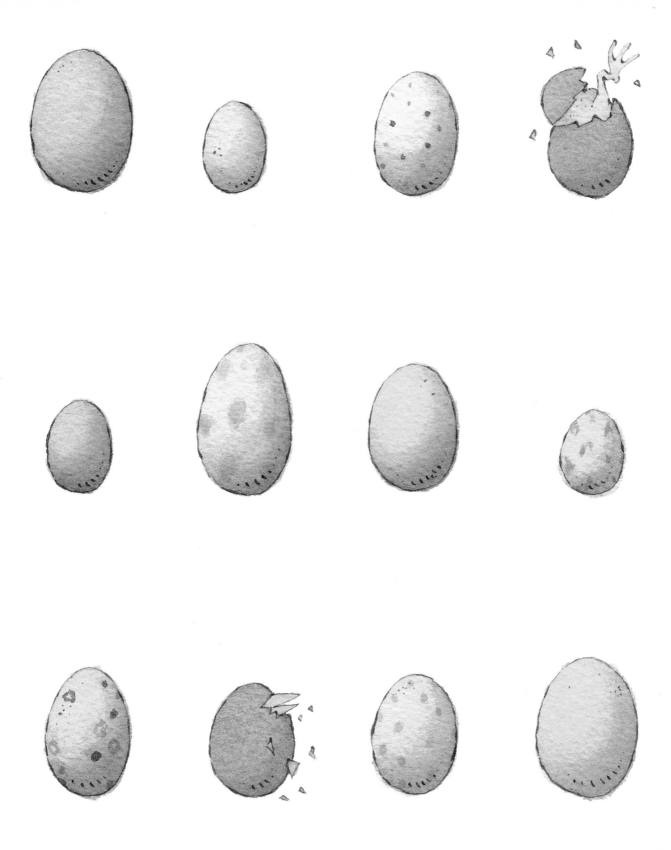